My Cat Is Sleeping

Written by Dee White

Illustrated by Tracie Grimwood

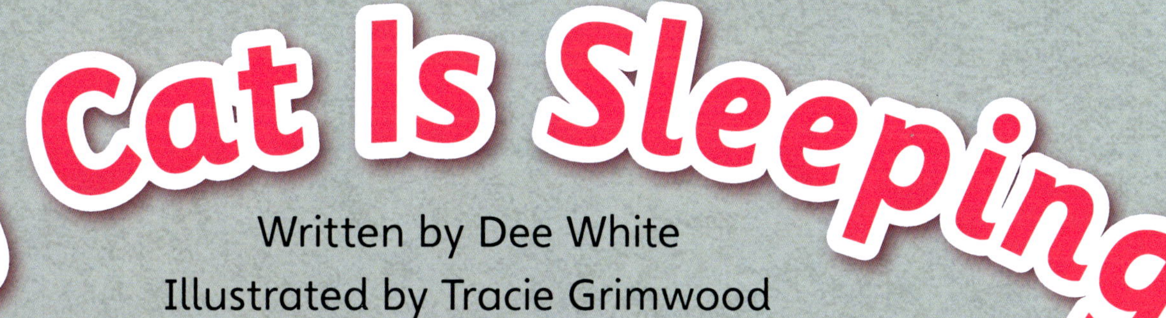

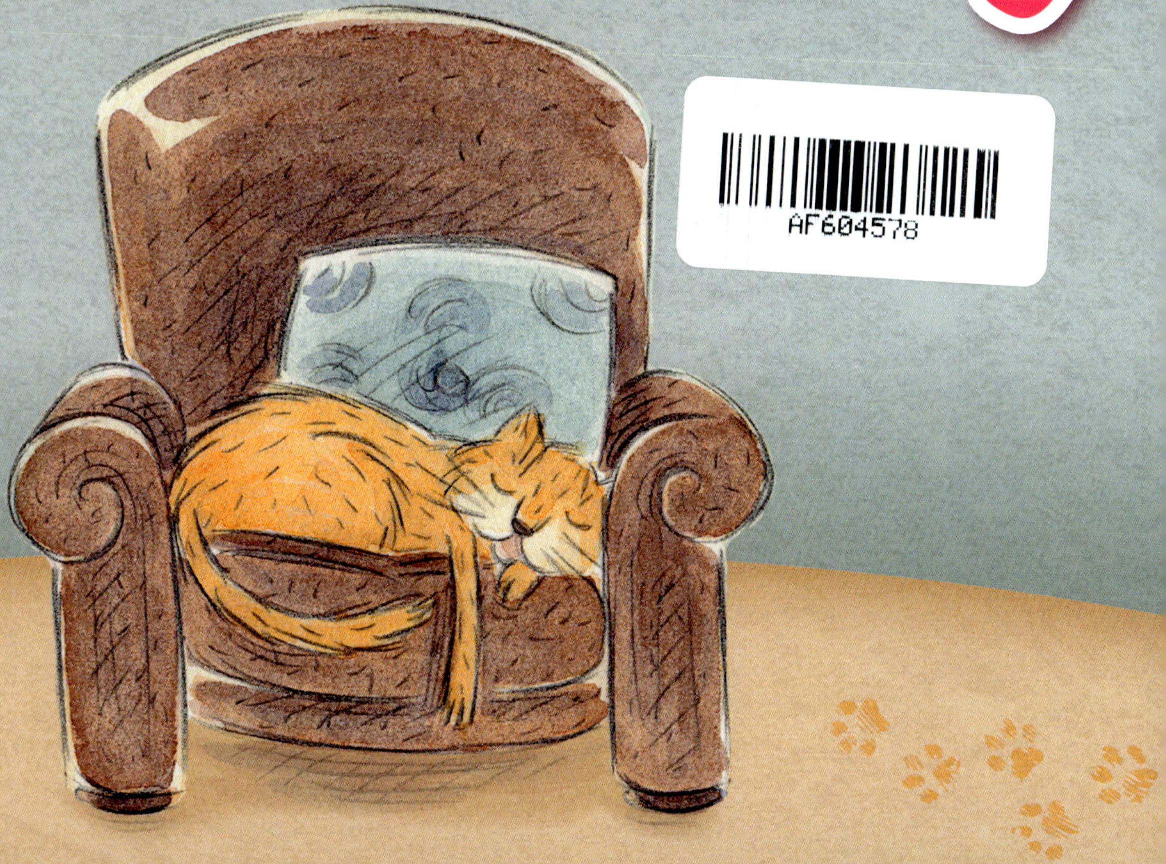

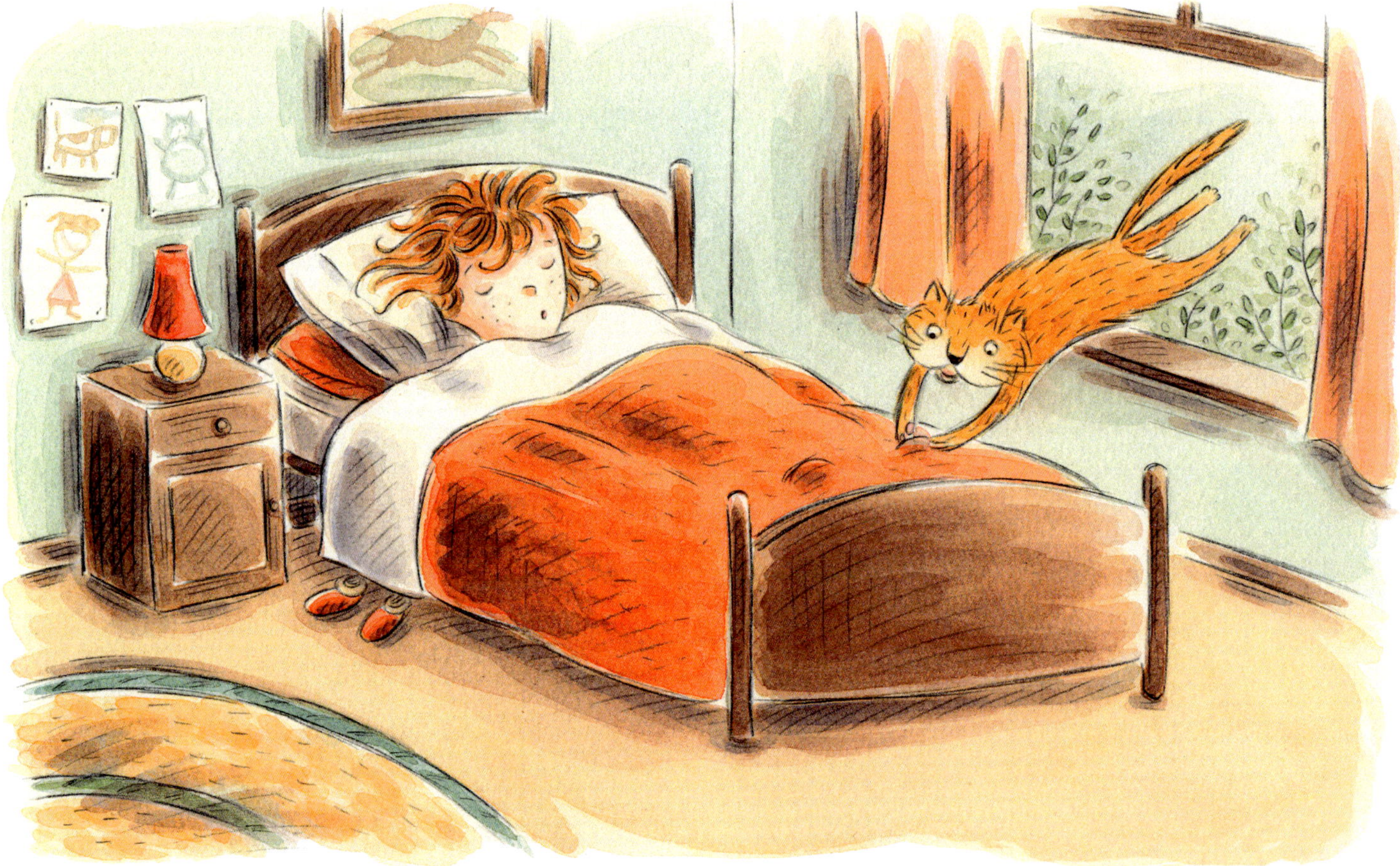

My cat is playing.

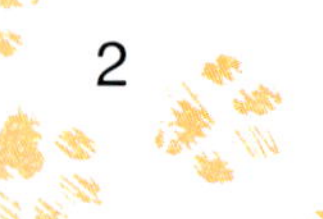

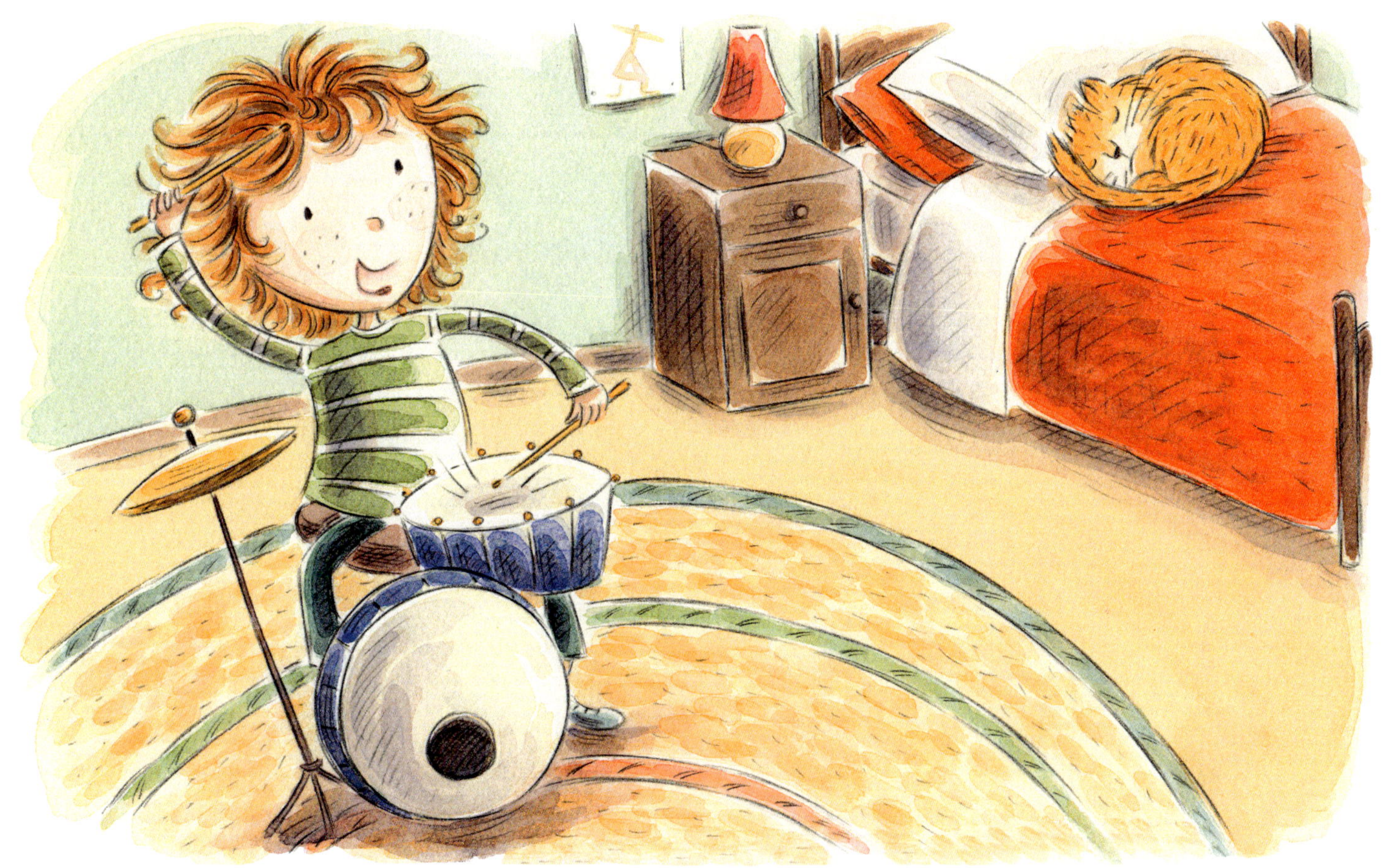

I am playing.

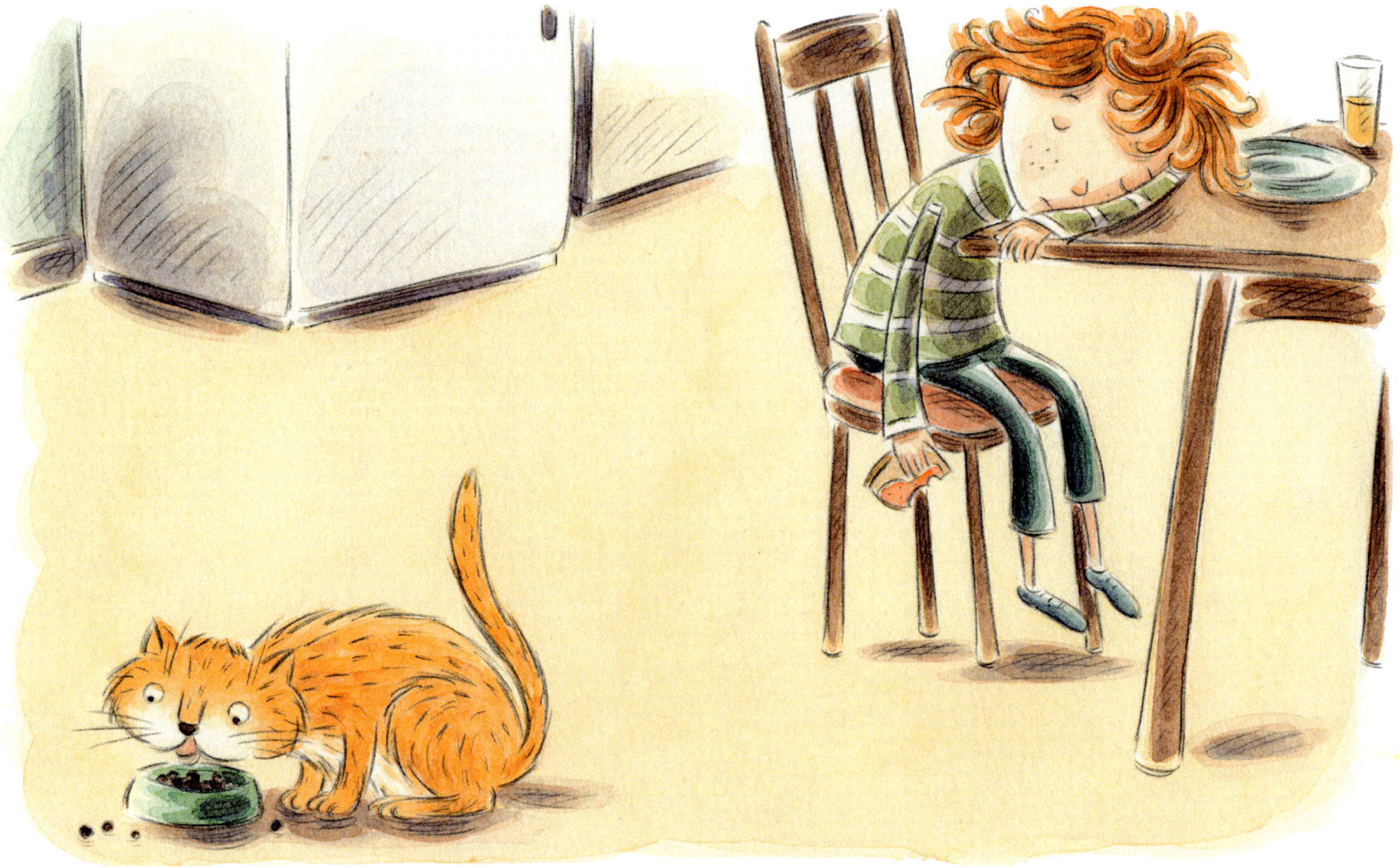

My cat is eating.

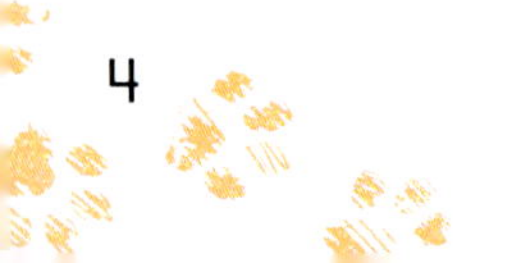

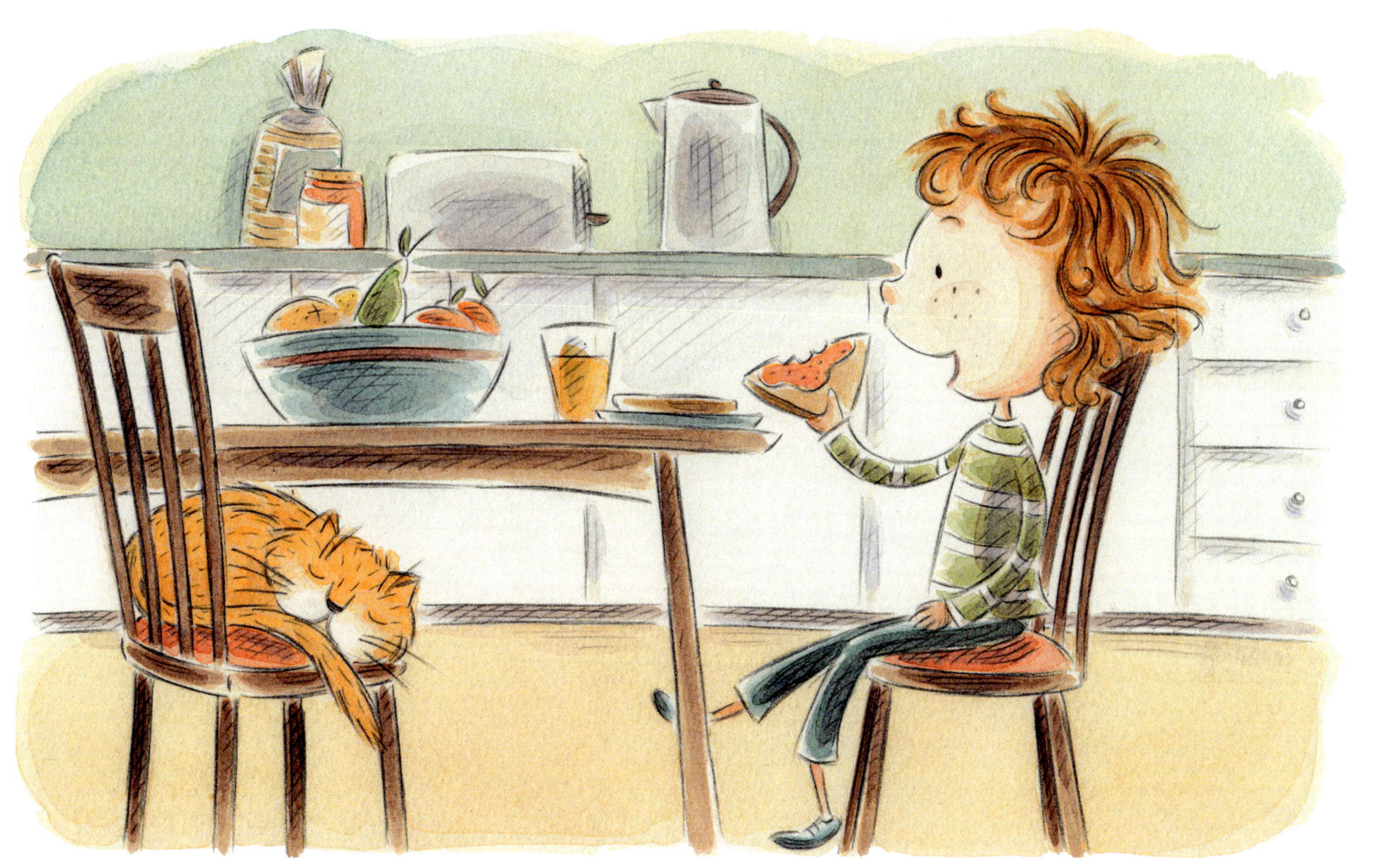

I am eating.

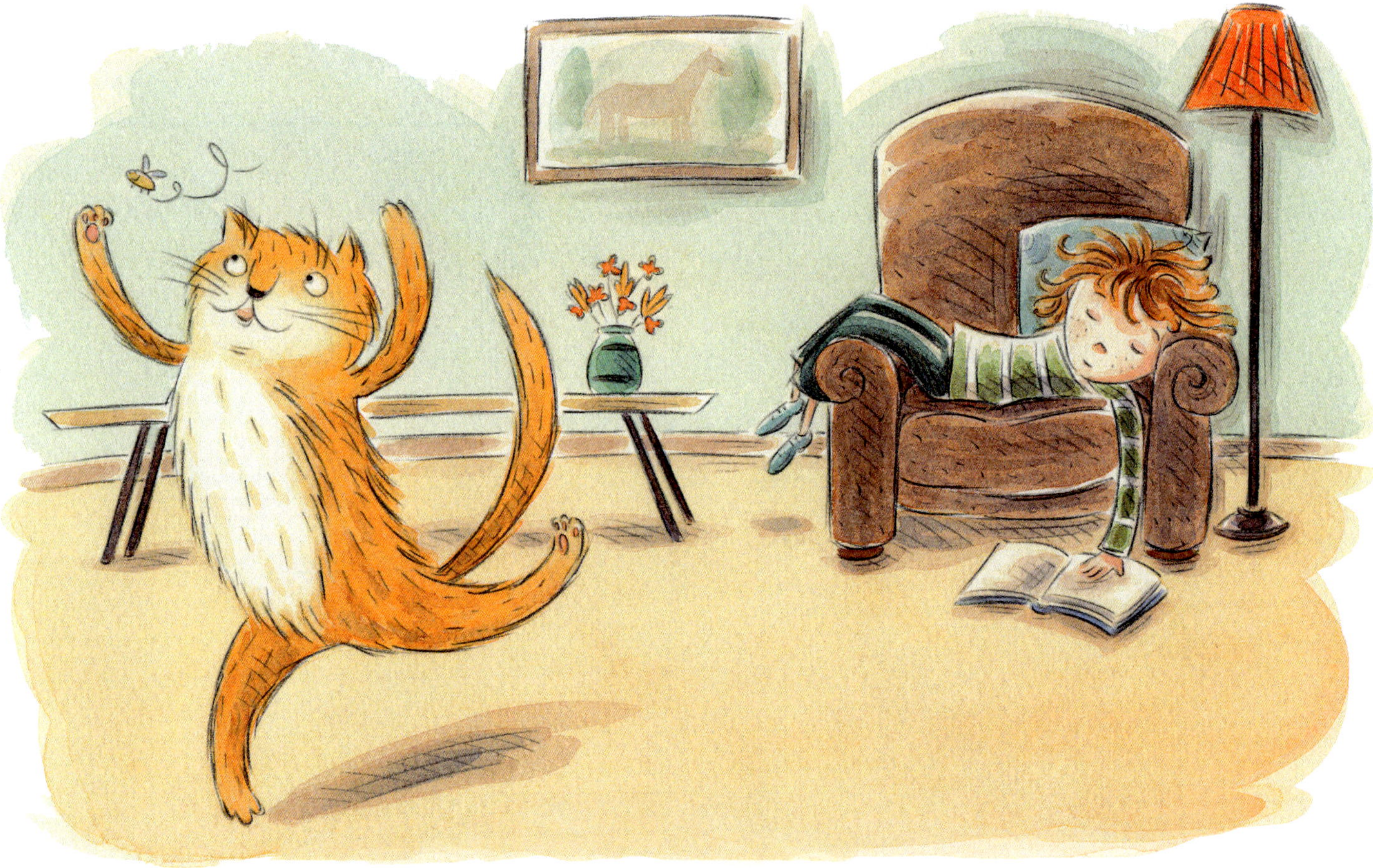

My cat is dancing.

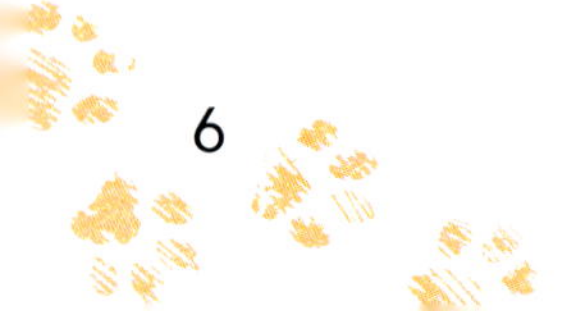

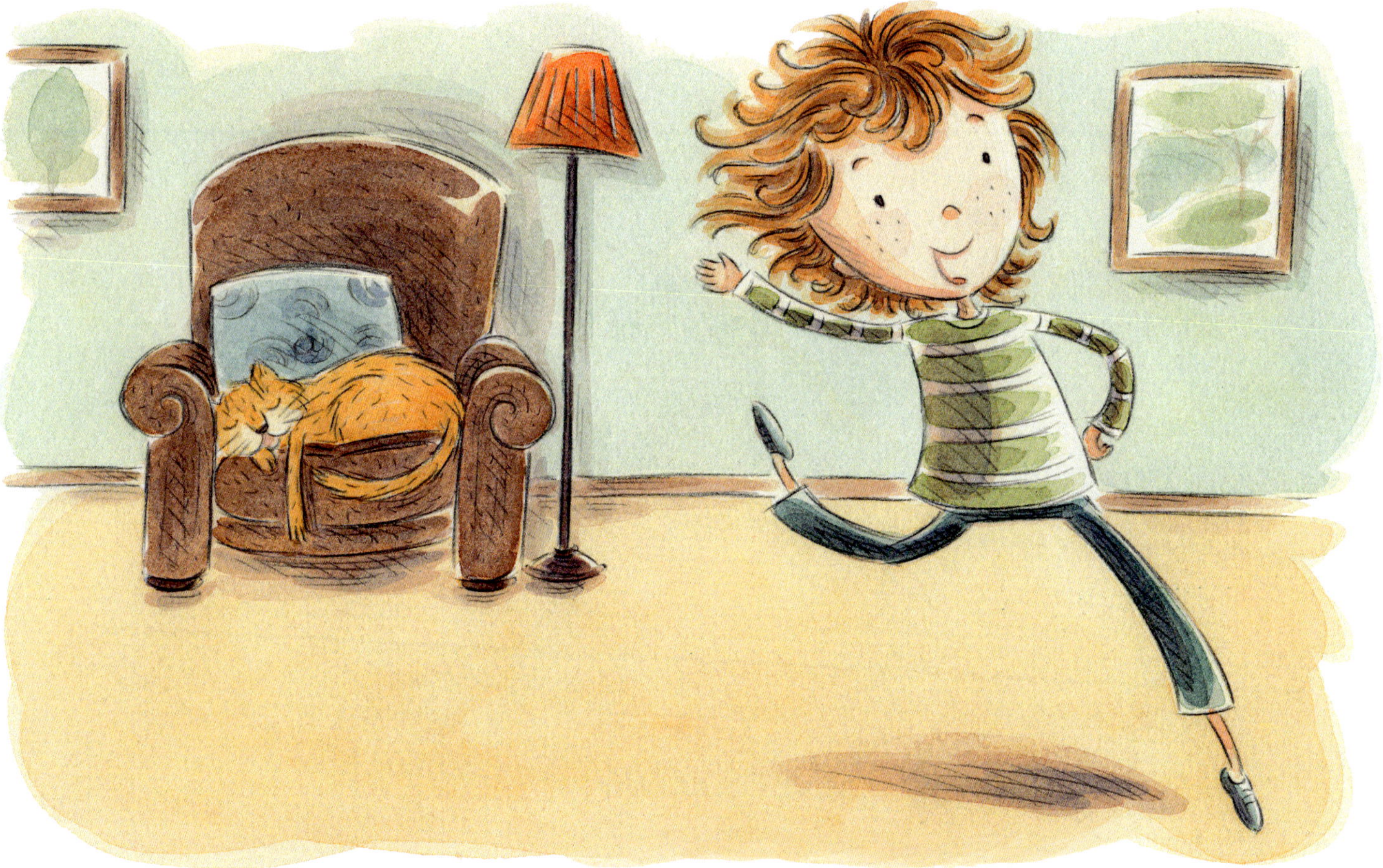

I am dancing.

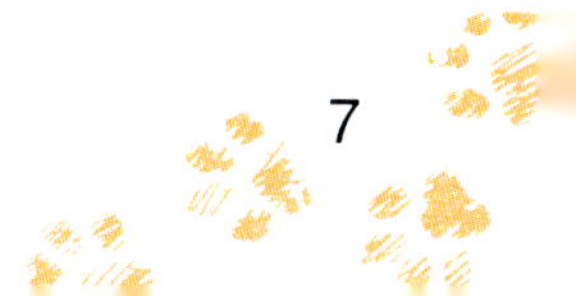

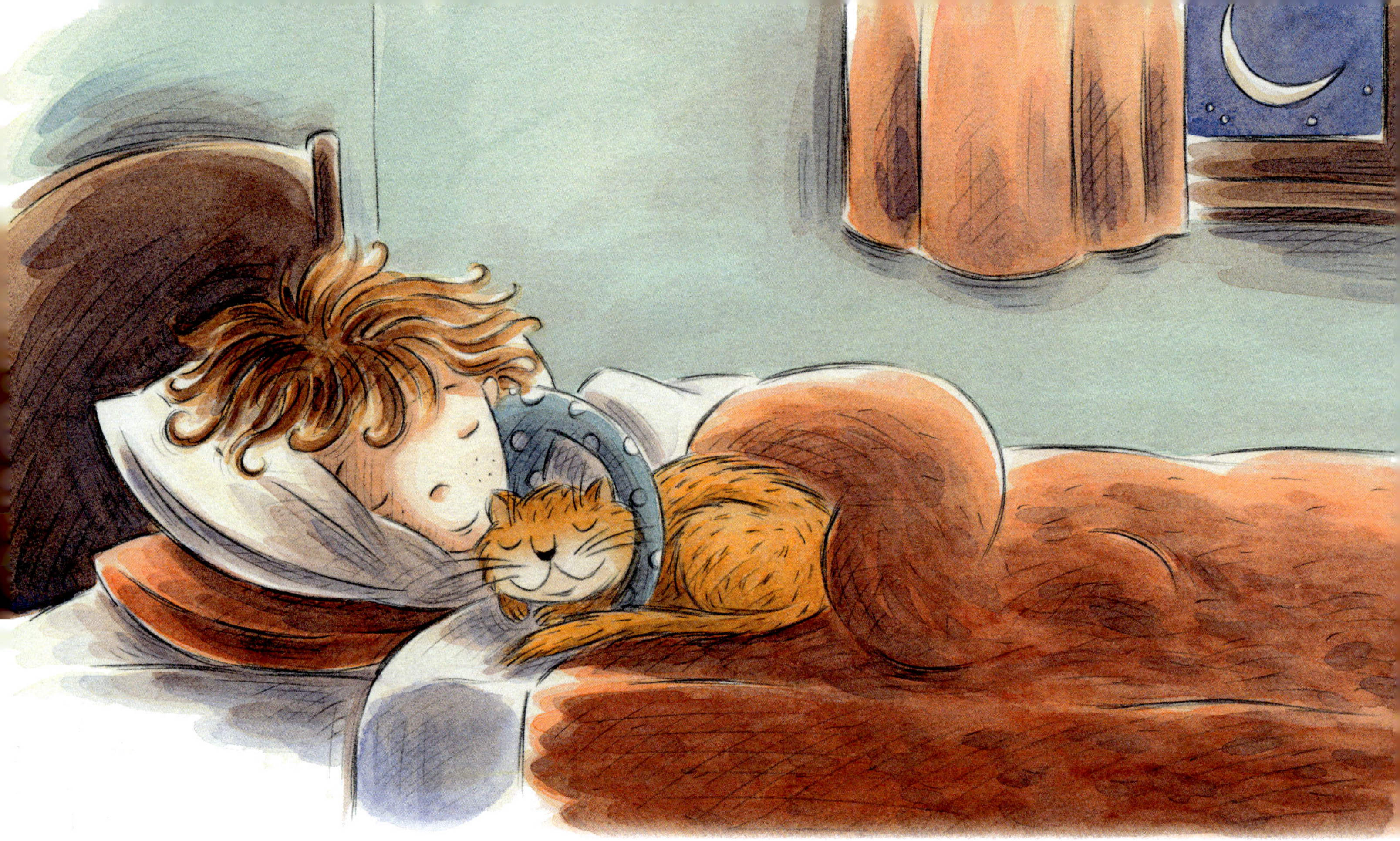

My cat is sleeping. I am sleeping too!

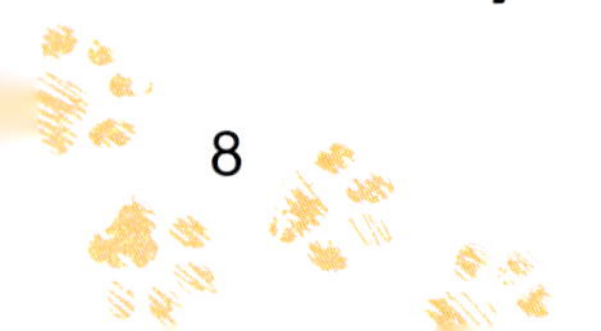